I Can Draw Animals

by Tony Tallarico

Little Simon

THIS BOOK IS DEDICATED TO—
Rex, Fido, Lassie, Kong, Black Beauty, Silver,
Rin-Tin-Tin, Rover, Spot, Flicka, Cheeta,
Champion, Nina, Anthony, Elvira,

and most of all to you _____.

Little Simon

Copyright © 1984 by Tony Tallarico
An imprint of Simon & Schuster Children's Publishing Division
1230 Avenue of the Americas
New York, New York 10020
ISBN: 0-689-81194-2
10 9 8 7 6 5 4 3

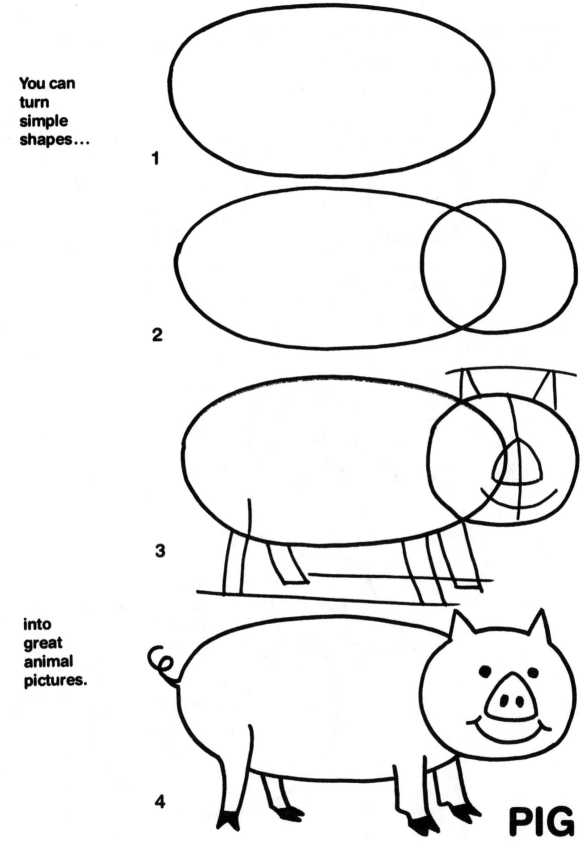

You can
turn
simple
shapes…

1

2

3

into
great
animal
pictures.

4

PIG

**Start by drawing the first five steps lightly in pencil.
Don't be surprised if you have to erase a lot, but make your corrections
and additions before erasing.**

1

Draw a
circle.

2

Add a
kite shape.

3

Add a
small circle.

4

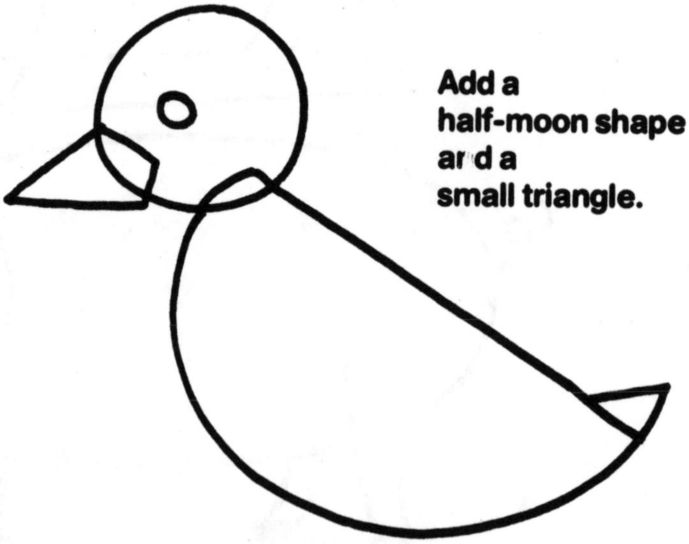

Add a
half-moon shape
and a
small triangle.

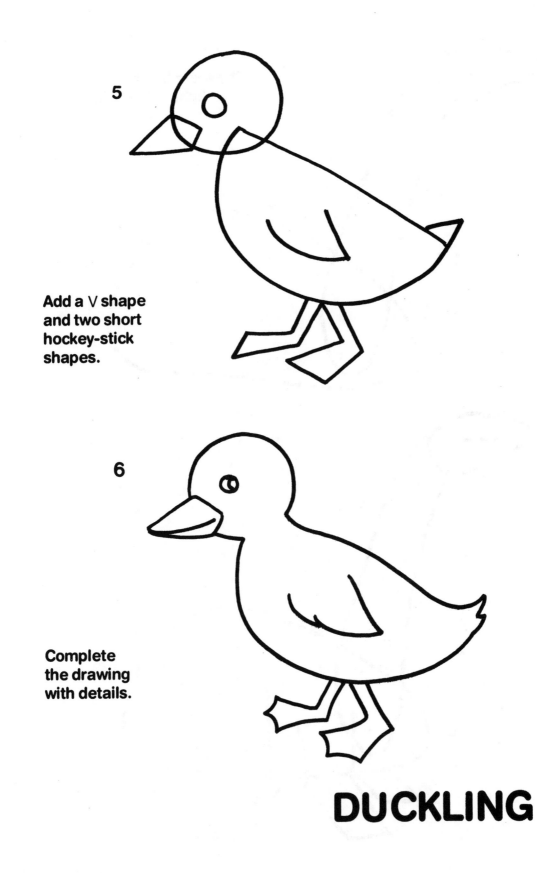

5

Add a V shape
and two short
hockey-stick
shapes.

6

Complete
the drawing
with details.

DUCKLING

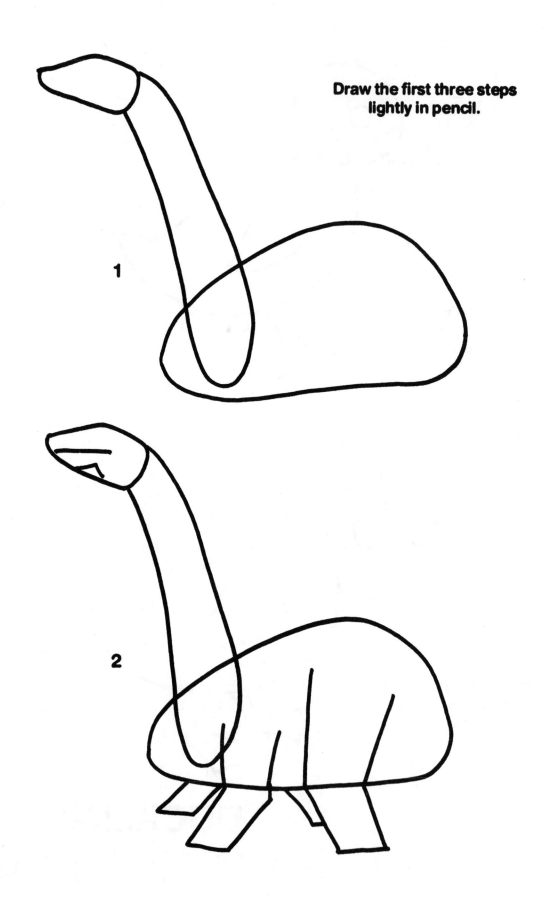

Draw the first three steps
lightly in pencil.

1

2

3

4

BRONTOSAURUS

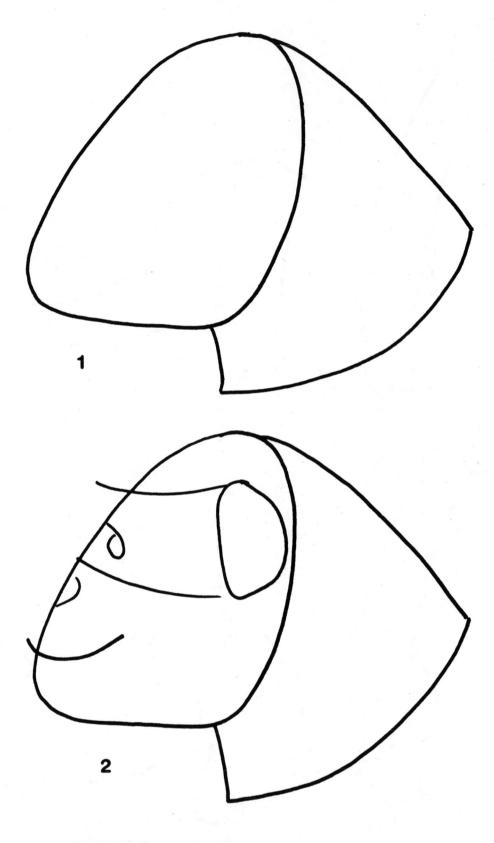

Draw the first two steps lightly in pencil.

3

CHIMPANZEE

ROOSTER

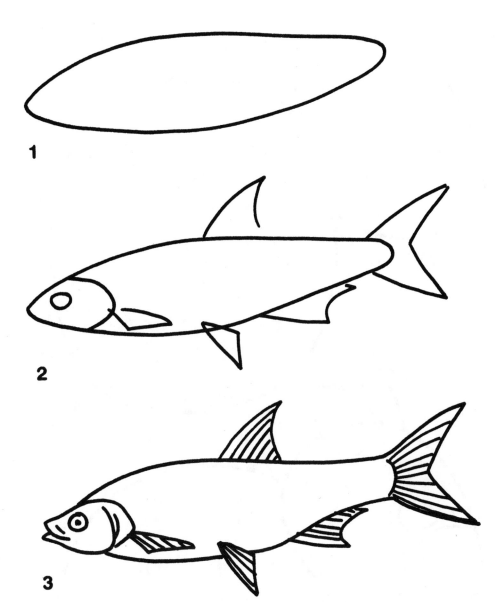

1

2

3

TROUT

1

2

3

GERBIL

1

2

3

GREYHOUND

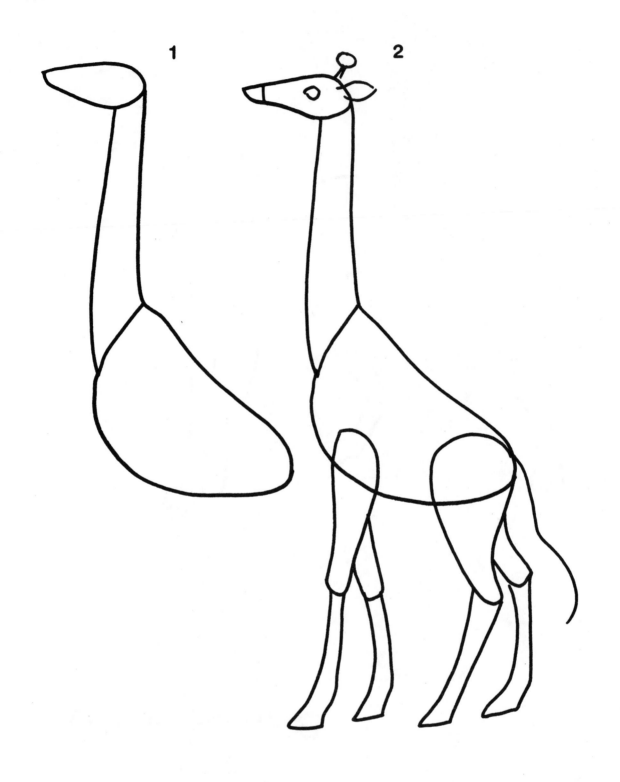

3

GIRAFFE

1

2

3

ELEPHANT

TRICERATOPS

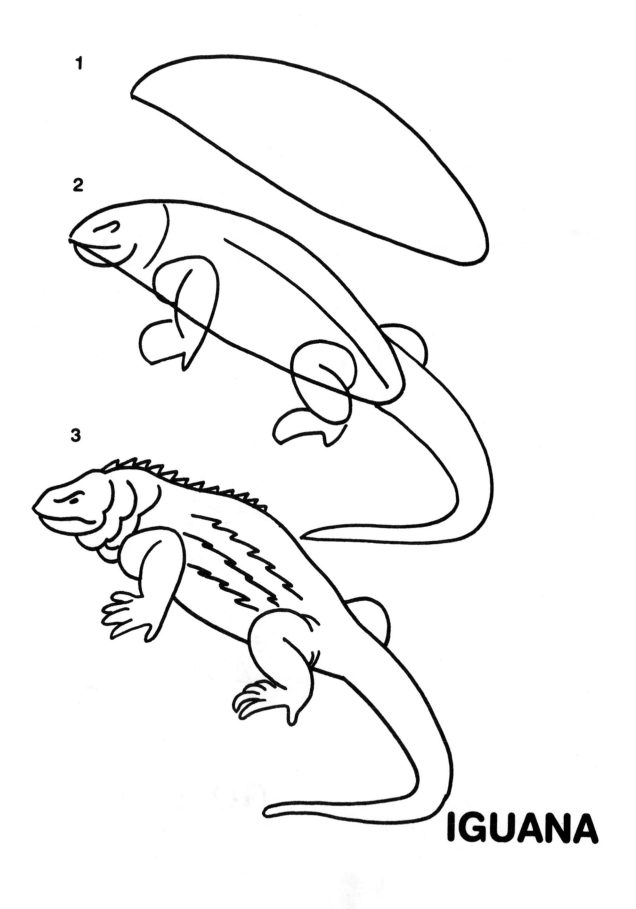

IGUANA

GOLDFISH

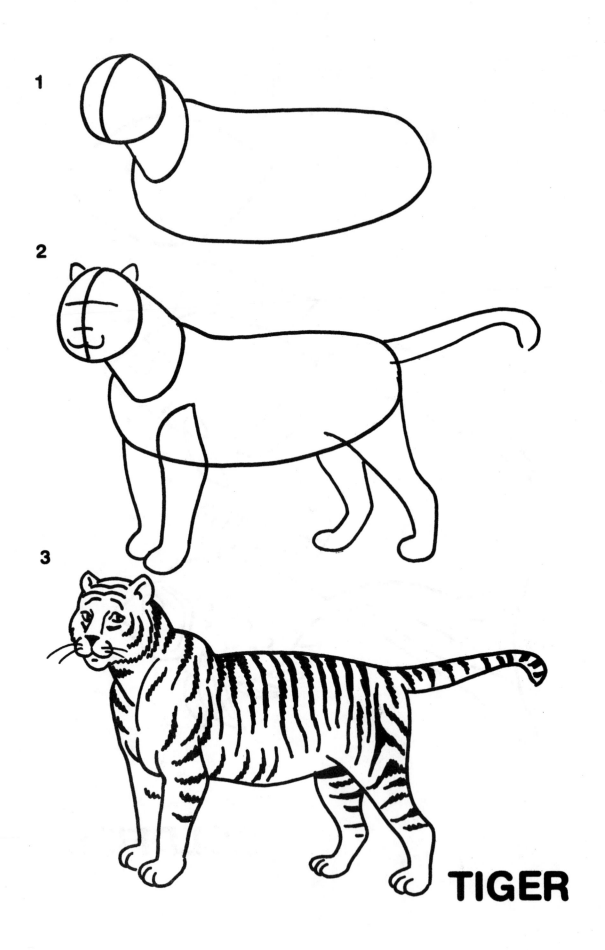

1

2

3

TIGER

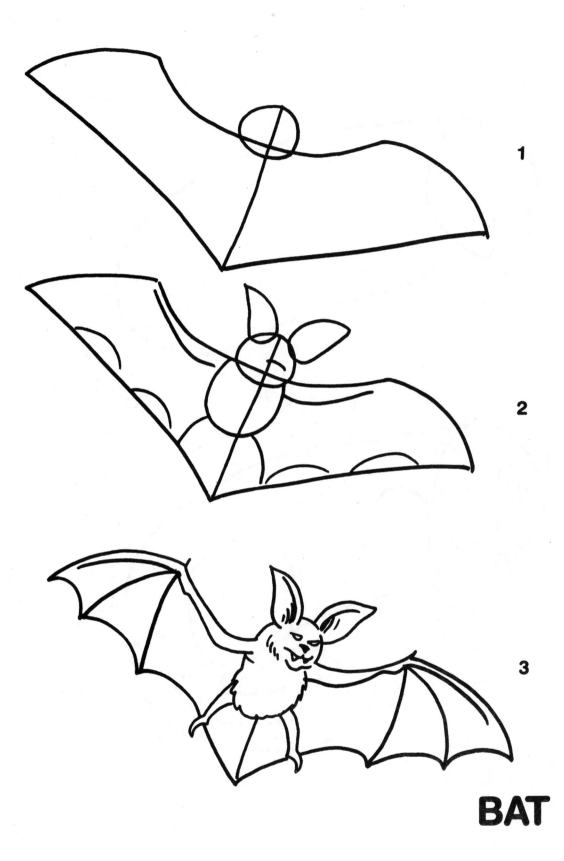

1

2

3

BAT

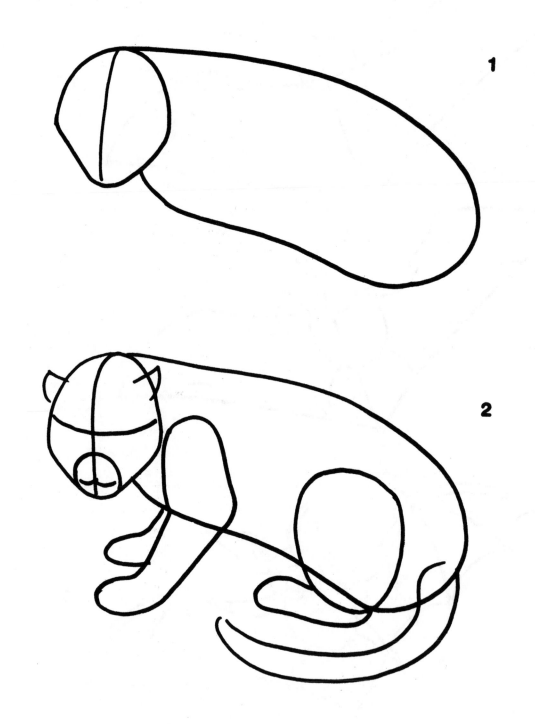

1

2

JAGUAR

PARROT

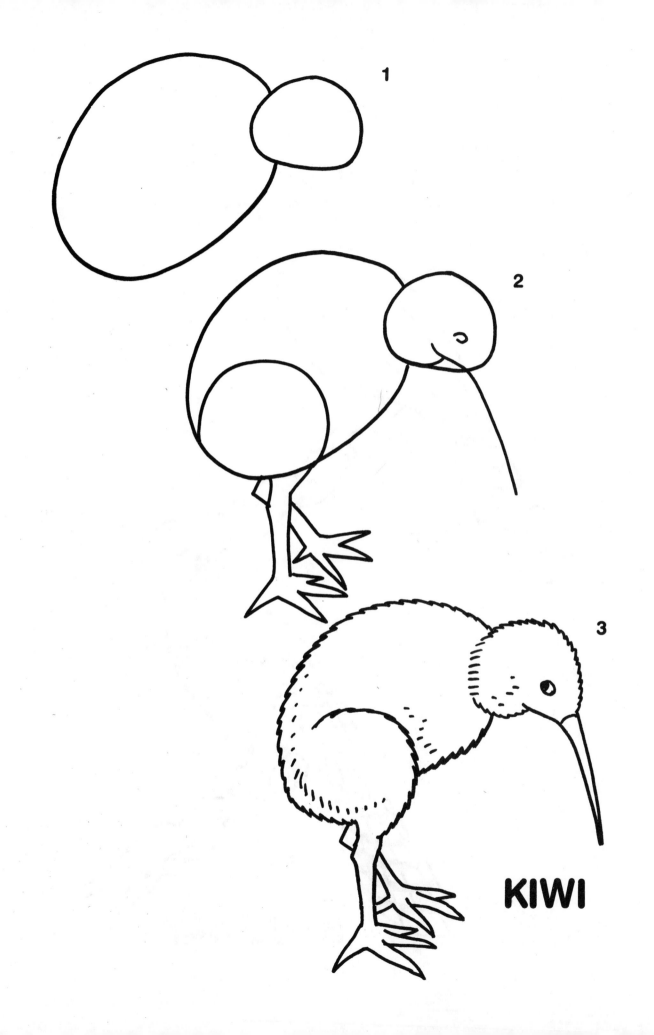

1

2

3

KIWI

BLUE JAY

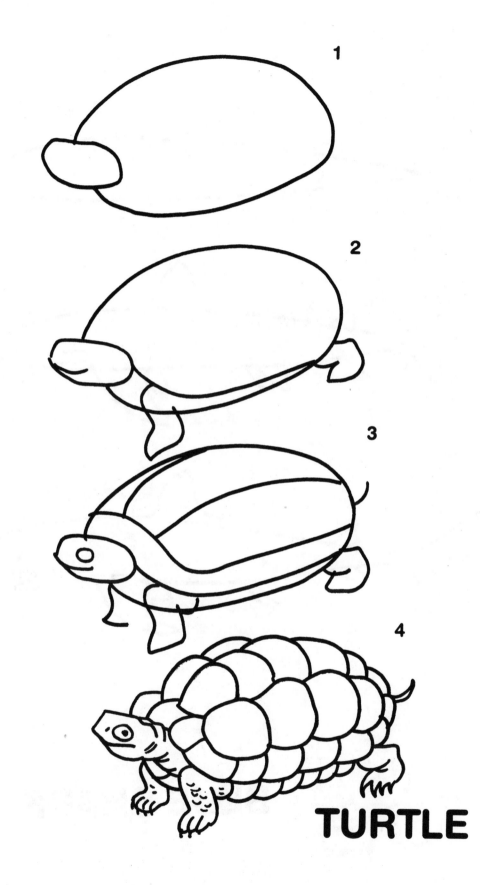

1

2

3

4

TURTLE

1

2

3

BLUE SHARK

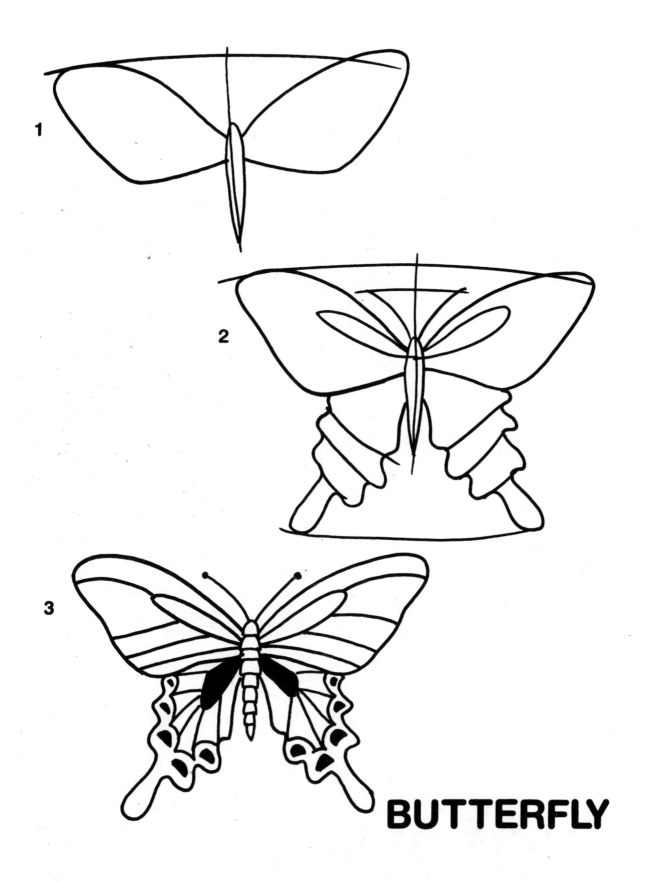

1

2

3

BUTTERFLY

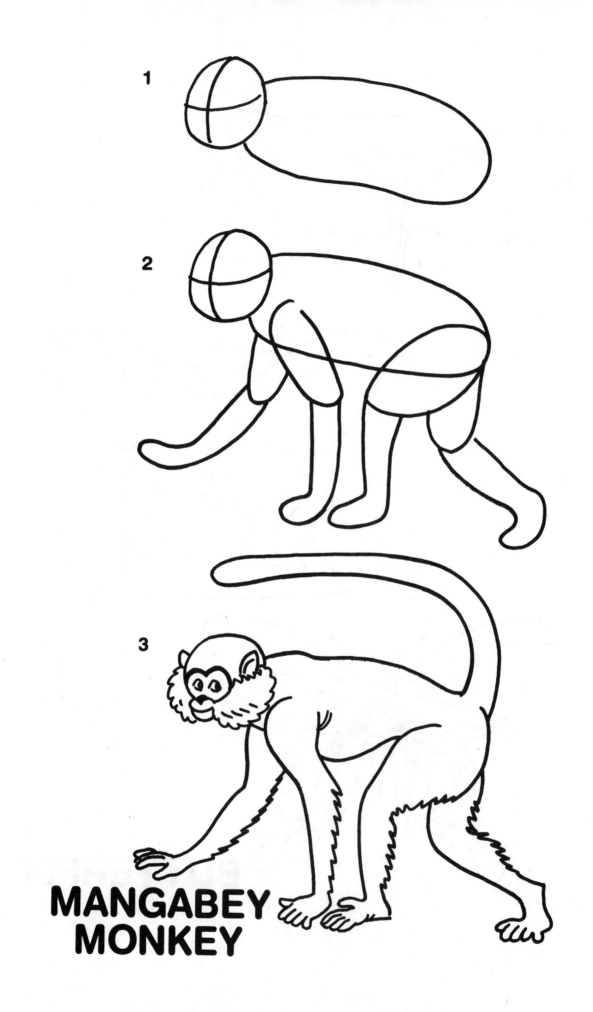

MANGABEY MONKEY

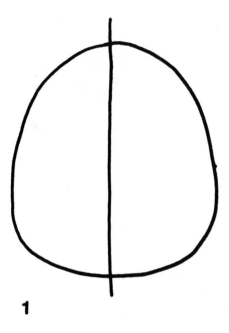

1

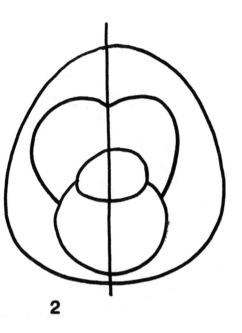

2

3

4

CHIMPANZEE

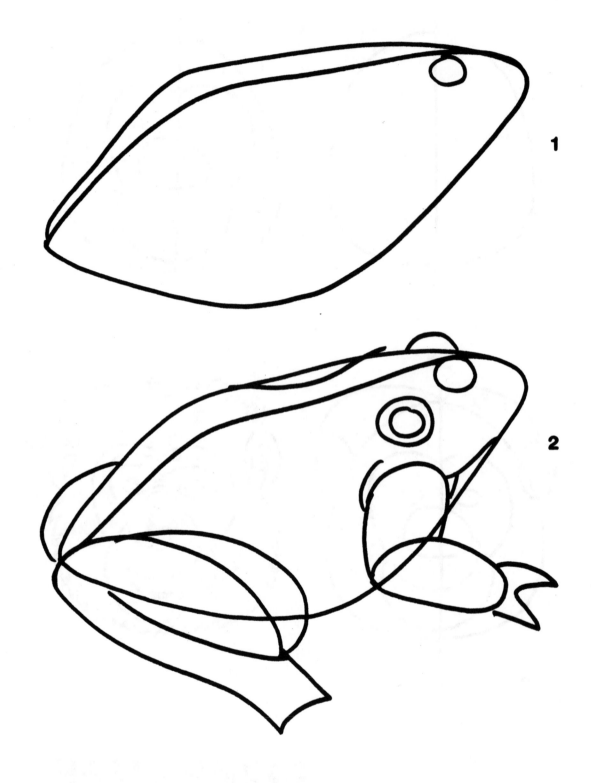

1

2

3

FROG

1

2

3

BEAR

1

2

3

HORSE

1

2

3

RHINOCEROS

1

2

3

RABBIT

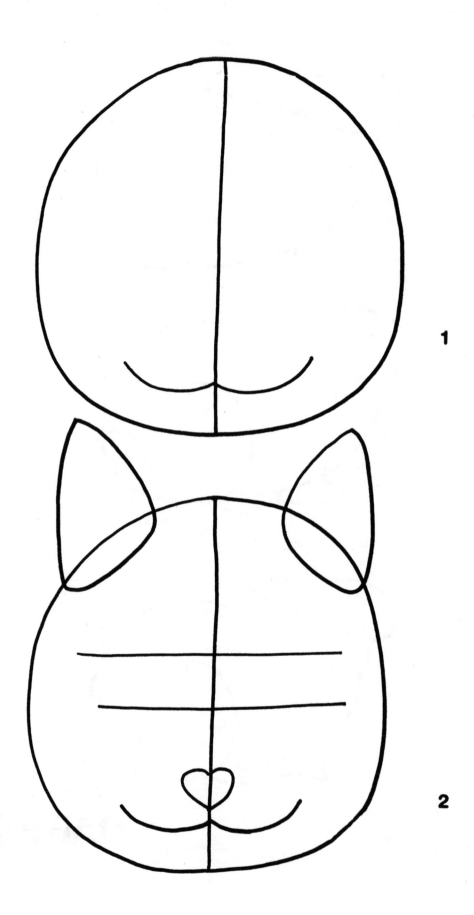

1

2

3

4

CAT

3

CAMEL

KANGAROO

1

2

3

SQUIRREL

1

2

3

BLOODHOUND

1

2

COLLIE DOG

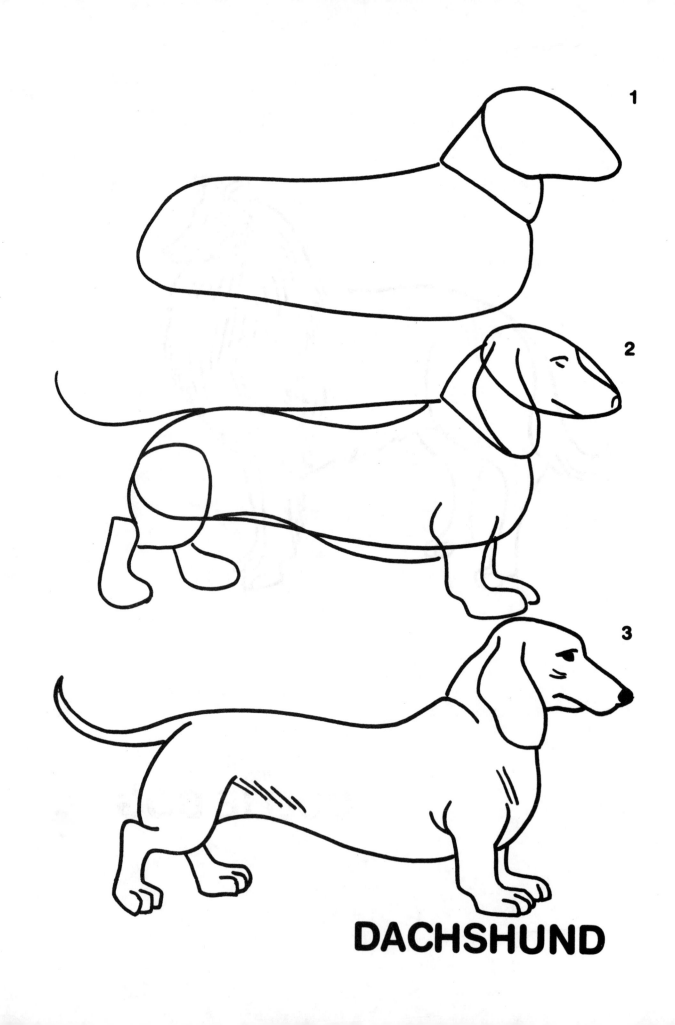

DACHSHUND

1

2

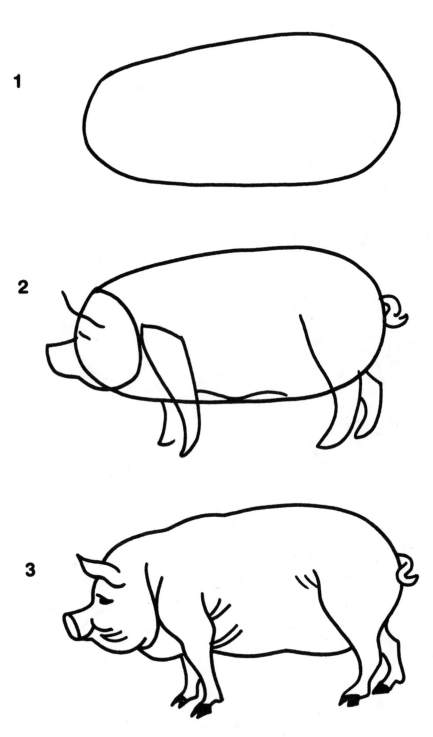

3

PIG

1

2

3

CAT

1

2

3

4

HORSE

1

2

3

FAWN

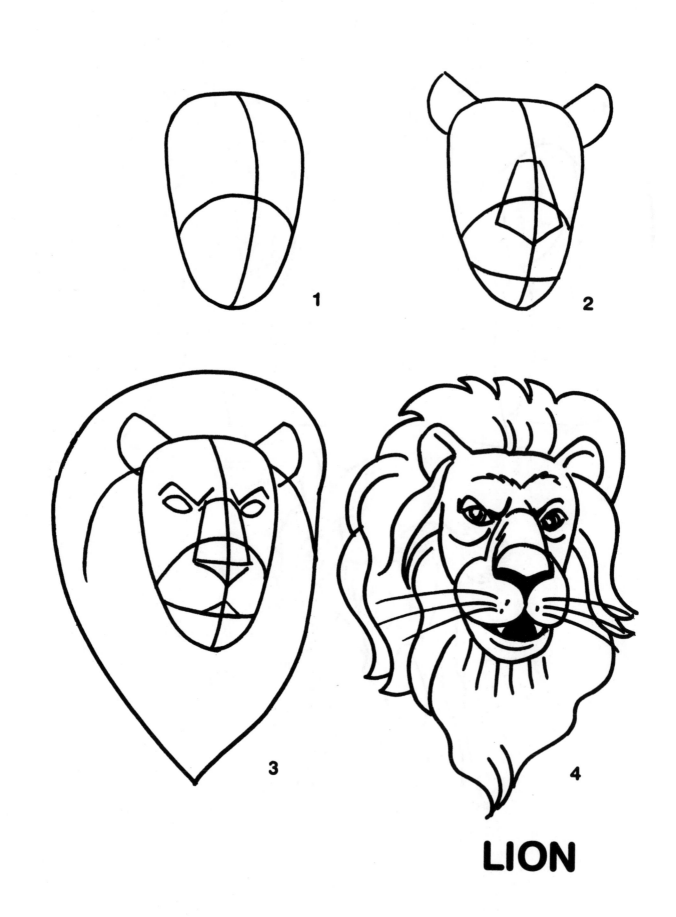

1

2

3

4

LION

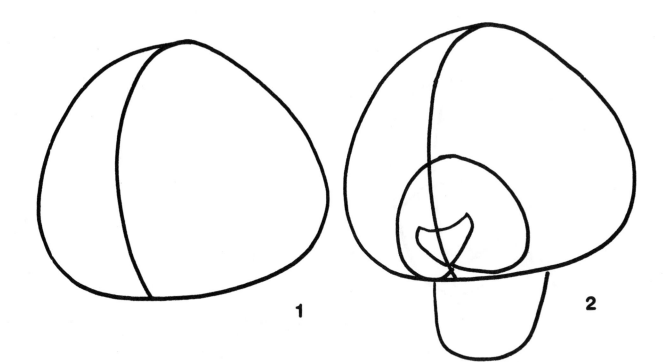

1

2

3

4

TIGER

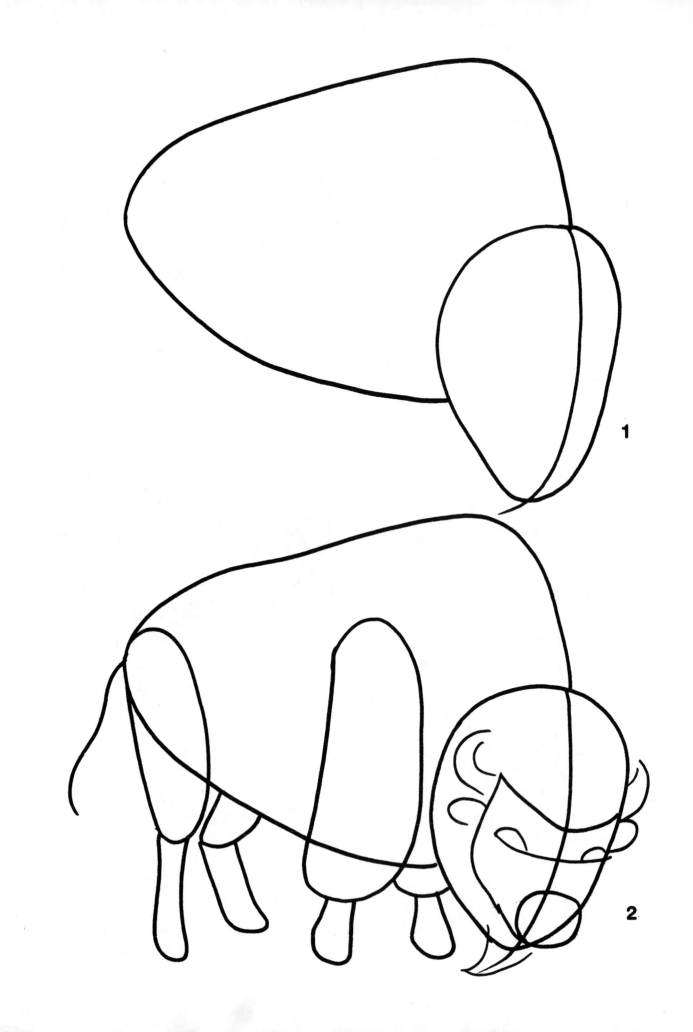

1

2

3

BISON—AMERICAN BUFFALO

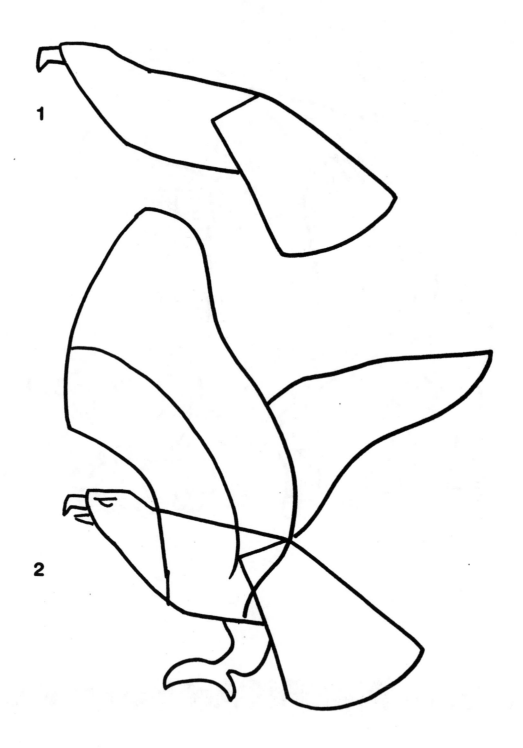

1

2

3

AMERICAN EAGLE

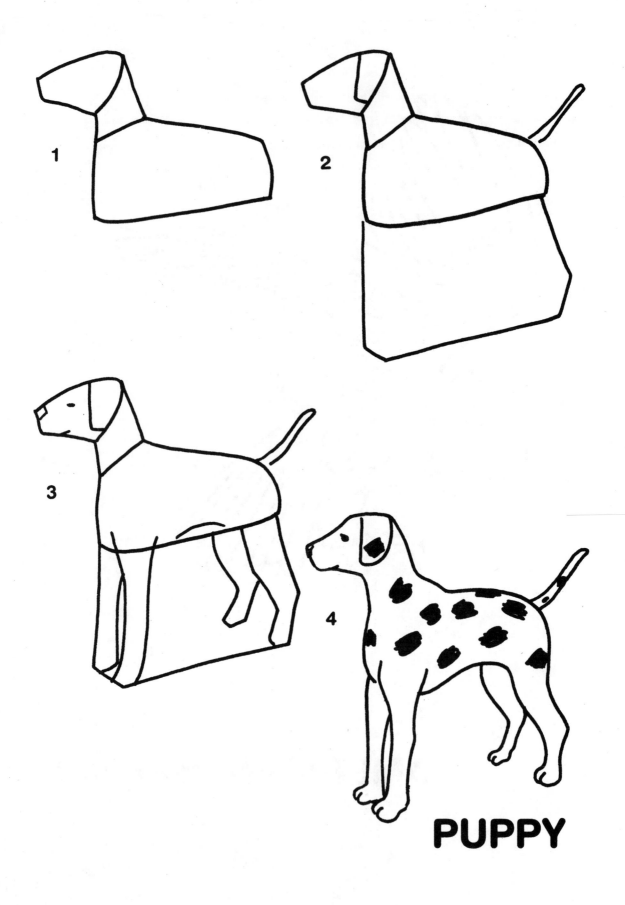

PUPPY